by Anna Kang   *illustrated by* Christopher Weyant

That's (Not) Mine

To our parents for their loving support
and for teaching us how to share.

two lions

Text copyright © 2015 by Anna Kang
Illustrations copyright © 2015 by Christopher Weyant

Published by Two Lions, New York
www.apub.com

Amazon, the Amazon logo, and Two Lions
are trademarks of Amazon.com, Inc., or its affiliates.

ISBN-13: 978-1-4778-2639-3 (hardcover)
ISBN-13: 978-1-4778-7638-1 (digital)

Design by Sara Gillingham Studio

The illustrations are rendered in ink and watercolor with brush pens on Arches paper.

Printed in China
First Edition
1 3 5 7 9 10 8 6 4 2

I was sitting in it before.

I'm sitting in it now.

FLING!